Dear Parent:
Your child's love of reading starts here!

Every child learns to read in a different way and at his or her own speed. Some go back and forth between reading levels and read favorite books again and again. Others read through each level in order. You can help your young reader improve and become more confident by encouraging his or her own interests and abilities. From books your child reads with you to the first books he or she reads alone, there are I Can Read Books for every stage of reading:

SHARED READING
Basic language, word repetition, and whimsical illustrations, ideal for sharing with your emergent reader

BEGINNING READING
Short sentences, familiar words, and simple concepts for children eager to read on their own

READING WITH HELP
Engaging stories, longer sentences, and language play for developing readers

READING ALONE
Complex plots, challenging vocabulary, and high-interest topics for the independent reader

ADVANCED READING
Short paragraphs, chapters, and exciting themes for the perfect bridge to chapter books

I Can Read Books have introduced children to the joy of reading since 1957. Featuring award-winning authors and illustrators and a fabulous cast of beloved characters, I Can Read Books set the standard for beginning readers.

A lifetime of discovery begins with the magical words **"I Can Read!"**

Visit www.icanread.com for information on enriching your child's reading experience.

bushes

seeds

flowers

snow

grass

sun

paintbrush

table

scooter

my little Pony

The Greenest Day

WITHDRAWN

by Jennifer Christie
illustrated by Lyn Fletcher

HARPER
An Imprint of HarperCollinsPublishers

Spring had arrived!

The  had melted.

The had turned green

and the was shining.

"Look at these !"

said Cheerilee.

Cheerilee put her

on the .

"The are beautiful!"

said Scootaloo from her .

"I'll paint the

so it can be pretty, too,"

added Toola-Roola happily.

But Cheerilee wasn't listening.

The 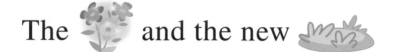 and the new

gave Cheerilee a good idea.

"Let's call today Green Day!"

she said.

"We can make Ponyville

look extra-pretty.

Let's find fun ways to reuse

what we already have."

"Here are some cans,"

Cheerilee said.

"You can turn them

into pots for

with a little paint!"

she said to Toola-Roola.

The ponies were happy.

All except Toola-Roola.

"Let's start planting the

and painting the flower pots,"

Cheerilee said.

"Painting was my idea,"

said Toola-Roola.

She held up her .

But Cheerilee was too busy

to hear her friend.

Toola-Roola put down

her .

"I have ideas, too,"

she said to Cheerilee.

Scootaloo came over

on her  to see

why Toola-Roola was upset.

Cheerilee put her  down

on the .

"Toola-Roola," said Cheerilee.

"I talked the whole time!"

Cheerilee felt terrible that

she hadn't let Toola-Roola speak.

"I'm so sorry," she said.

"That's okay, Cheerilee,"

Toola-Roola said.

"Let's all share our ideas!"

Cheerilee looked happy.

"Should we plant

near the ?" she asked.

"I'll use the cans you found

for the pots," said Toola-Roola.

The ponies were excited

about their first Green Day.

"I found some leftover paint!"

said Cheerilee.

Toola-Roola smiled.

"I can use that paint for the

," she said to Cheerilee.

Toola-Roola painted the .

Cheerilee planted .

Scootaloo watered the .

"I made my watering can

from an old milk bottle!"

Scootaloo said proudly.

At last, Ponyville sparkled.

Cheerilee gave Toola-Roola .

"I love Green Day.

Let's do it again!" said Toola-Roola.